Walt Disney's
PINOCCHIO

ILLUSTRATIONS BY THE WALT DISNEY STUDIO

ADAPTED BY CAMPBELL GRANT

FROM THE WALT DISNEY MOTION PICTURE "PINOCCHIO"

Based on the Story by Collodi

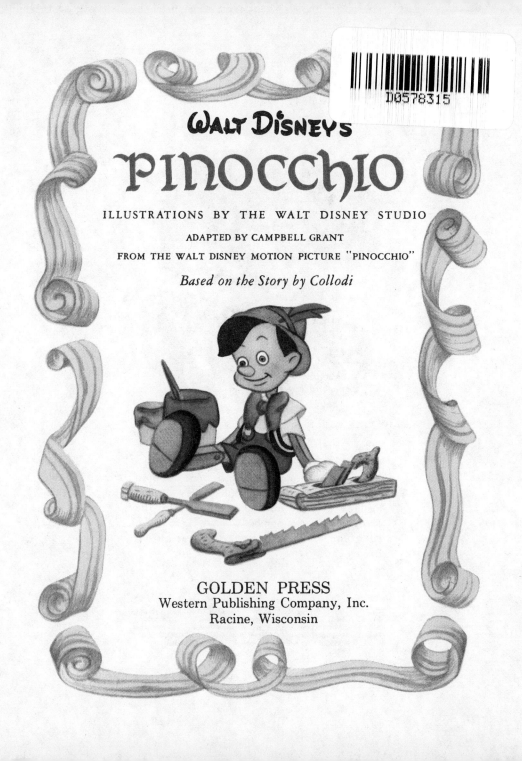

GOLDEN PRESS
Western Publishing Company, Inc.
Racine, Wisconsin

This Little Golden Book was produced under the supervision of

THE WALT DISNEY STUDIO

Little Golden Books here bring you, in gay color, delightful stories and illustrations adapted from the world-famous Walt Disney Motion Pictures. In them you will find *Pinocchio, The Three Little Pigs, Bambi, Dumbo, Cinderella, Peter Pan,* as well as many other well-loved Disney characters.

KINDLY Old Geppetto stood at his work-bench and carved on a puppet that looked just like a real boy. He sang as he worked, and Little Figaro, his cat, played with the chips as they fell from his knife. Jiminy Cricket chirped merrily on the hearth, and the goldfish, Cleo, swam around and around in her bowl.

"There," said Geppetto, as he held up the puppet, "you're finished."

He held the strings and danced the little wooden boy across the floor.

"How I wish you were a real live boy!" he said. "What fun we would have, you and Figaro and Cleo and I!"

"What about me?" asked a small voice. "Couldn't I have fun, too?"

"Ho, Jiminy Cricket! Of course you could have fun, too," laughed Geppetto. "You could go everywhere with him to keep him out of trouble. What shall we call him . . . Pinocchio? Little, wooden-headed Pinocchio."

"A dandy name, Pinocchio!" cried Jiminy Cricket. He jumped from the floor to the workbench. "A dandy name!"

At that moment all the clocks in the house started to strike. Old Geppetto looked up.

"It's nine o'clock," he said. "Time for sleep."

He placed Pinocchio on the workbench, tumbled Figaro into the big bed, and blew a kiss to Cleo in her bowl. He opened the window, and the light of the Evening Star streamed into the room.

"Star light, star bright...," he said softly. "I wish Pinocchio were a real, live boy!"

He looked once more at the merry little puppet and then settled down in his bed. In a moment he was snoring.

Only Jiminy Cricket was still awake. He was unhappy, thinking Old Geppetto would never have his

wish. Suddenly he heard strange, sweet music. The Evening Star sailed down through the sky, and into Geppetto's window. The cottage was filled with dazzling light, and there stood a lovely fairy dressed all in blue.

"It's the Blue Fairy!" whispered Jiminy Cricket. "Geppetto will get his wish this time, or my name isn't Jiminy Cricket!"

The Blue Fairy flew to the workbench where little wooden Pinocchio sat, and said:

Awake, Pinocchio, and live!
To you the gift of life I give.
Be good, and bring Geppetto joy,
And grow to be a real, live boy.

You can imagine Geppetto's surprise the next morning, when he found Pinocchio running around!

"I'm dreaming! You can't be alive! You're still made of wood!" said the astonished old man.

"But if I'm brave and good, I'll be a real live boy some day," said Pinocchio joyfully.

At last Geppetto said, "Now, Pinocchio, it's time for all good boys to go to school." And Pinocchio started out.

"Pinoke!" Jiminy Cricket called. "Wait for me!"

But although the Blue Fairy had told Pinocchio that Jiminy Cricket was to be his friend and conscience, Pinocchio did not hear the voice of his little friend.

Suddenly, something tripped Pinocchio. It was a cane, thrust between his flying feet by the sly old fox J. Worthington Foulfellow.

Foulfellow helped Pinocchio to his feet and winked at his partner Gideon, the bad cat.

"Ha ha, Pinocchio," began Foulfellow, "you were going a little too fast! A little too fast, and in the *wrong* direction. Now I have a plan for you. Come. . . ."

"But I'm on my way to school," said Pinocchio.
"To school? Nonsense!" said Foulfellow. "I have
a much better plan."

The three of them set off, arm in arm, and Jiminy Cricket came panting along behind.

Soon they came to a great coach. The two scoundrels took from the wicked-looking coachman a large bag. They had sold Pinocchio for gold! Then they went away laughing.

Jiminy was frightened, but he hopped bravely aboard just as the coach drove off.

The coach was pulled by six sad little donkeys. It was filled with boys of all sizes and ages, a noisy, rowdy lot. Pinocchio made friends with the leader, a loud boy named Lampwick. But Jiminy sadly hid in a corner. He knew this was not good!

Pleasure Island was wonderful—just as Foulfellow had said. And when Jiminy Cricket tried to get Pinocchio to go home, Pinocchio turned his back on his tiny friend.

"I'll go back after a while," he said. "Right now
I want some fun!"

"You bet!" yelled Lampwick. "Come on!"

Every day they played. They ate candy and ice

cream and cake and more candy. They broke windows, and threw mud, and carved up furniture.

"Good," said the Mayor. "Go to it, boys!"

"Fine," cried the Coachman. "They're almost ready!"

"Pinocchio!" begged Jiminy Cricket. "Please come with me!"

"Who's the goody-goody?" sneered Lampwick.

"Yah," Pinocchio said, "go away, Cricket! I'm tired of you!"

He looked at Lampwick for approval. Right before his eyes, Lampwick's ears became long and fuzzy . . . then he grew a tail . . . and then, in a twinkling of an eye, Lampwick turned into a little donkey!

The Coachman came running and put a rope around Lampwick's neck.

"Aha!" he cried, "another donkey to sell to the man who runs the salt mines!"

He reached for Pinocchio, because Pinocchio was growing donkey's ears and a donkey's tail, too. But Jiminy Cricket shouted:

"Run, Pinocchio! Come on!"

And *this* time Pinocchio ran with Jiminy Cricket. They ran to the edge of the island and dived into the water and swam away from that terrible place.

Hours later, wet and tired, they came to Geppetto's

cottage. But no one was there. Old Geppetto had taken Figaro and Cleo and gone to search for Pinocchio. Poor Pinocchio!

"It's all my fault," he told Jiminy Cricket. "Will I ever find my father again?"

"I don't know," said Jiminy. "It might be dangerous."

"I don't mind," declared Pinocchio. "It's my job to find him, even if it is dangerous."

So away went Pinocchio, with Jiminy beside him. And what adventures they did have! Up hill, down dale, into danger and out again!

They even chased a whale to the bottom of the sea. And the Blue Fairy watched them all the way. She was watching when they found Geppetto at last, and led him safely home.

It was only then that Geppetto noticed Pinocchio's donkey ears.

"I'm sorry, Father," Pinocchio said humbly. "But I do know better now."

Suddenly the Evening Star brightened the room, and the Blue Fairy appeared.

"You have learned your lesson well, Pinocchio," she said. And as her magic wand touched him, Pinocchio felt himself turn into a Real Boy!

"Father!" he cried, "I'm a real boy at last!"

Geppetto hugged him and laughed and cried for joy. And as for Jiminy Cricket, the Fairy gave him a badge of gold. And on the badge it said:

Awarded to a Good Conscience
who helped make
a Real Boy out of a Wooden Head.